# Subway Rider

**To order additional copies of this book, contact:**
Xlibris Corporation
1-888-795-4274
www.Xlibris.com
Orders@Xlibris.com
66220

# Subway Rider

Jason Ward

# INTRODUCTION

First let me tell you this is not for kids! or people that are shy about sex. This story will take you to a forbidden place, all of us think about, but most are afraid to go. It's about the New York Subway System and how much sex goes on right under your feet. Just think, if you are the type of person that might enjoy some people watching you have sex, what better place for you to go and fuck. Hey! It's not like you have to pay a lot, it's just $2 and you can ride all day. There are nine different colored trains, and miles of tunnels and storage places. It's like the cheapest motel in town.

It's the best way to see all of what New York has to offer, that's not on the tour guide! Let me give you a little taste of what you will read, if you so choose to purchase this book. First up, there are no names, I didn't want people to take this book too seriously. I made it so that you could let the freak out of you, if only in your mind. And live vicariously through my nasty, dirty, little thoughts. With that said, there is this guy on the crowded train, six foot two a hundred an fifty pounds of man muscle. With a leather trench coat, some black Timberland boots, a long shirt, and some blue jeans. He stands by the pole and waits for a woman to put her hand on the pole.

It's tight, so a little bump is expected, but this guy, had a plan when he left the house this morning. With his dick out of his pants, he bumps her hand with his dick. The next stop comes, and more people get on! He rubs her hand a little harder, and starts to grow. She's facing him so there's no way she doesn't know what he's doing. He's rock hard now, and rubbing his dick on her hand like he was fucking it. She could feel his hunk of man meat pulsating, so she did what any other freak ass women would do. She looked deep into his eyes and grabbed his dick, and squeezed it until he came. I mean it was the mother load! All up her sleeve, on her hand, her skirt and her shoes.

She thinks to herself, a nut like that had to be a, I just got out of jail nut. You think a bitch could get a, I just got out of jail fuck? She played with his dick until he got off the train and when he did she was right behind him. Not for nothing but I helped you get yours, now can you help me get mines? Now if this type of stuff you find enjoyable, please read on and tell me what you think of my freaky ass book!

# 1

The name of this story is subway rider! A true-fiction tale about what goes on, in our subway system.

Let's talk about our first person the every day rider, you know the one that seems to like the hustle and bustle of a crowded train. The one who doesn't care about bad breath, smelly bums, crying babies, or that annoying announcement that everybody hears, but can't understand.

This guy is o.k. with it, because he's not on his way to work, or on his way home, he is where he wants to be. On a crowded train filled with people so occupied they don't even see the predator next to them. He is a man hard to notice, blue or black suit on, sometimes a paper, other times a briefcase, always on the search for the perfect RUB DOWN!

His preparation starts in the morning, he shaves, showers, and picks his clothes out, just like you and me. He puts on some lotion, can't be dry, then his socks and T-shirt. Now at this point, he does something a little different. He puts his pants on with out any underwear at all! For a better feel, and I'm not talking about his clothes. O.k. he's ready to go to work, yeah the kind of work that gets your dick hard! He chooses what train to ride based on who he wants to get his rub on with. It's like this: the # 4 train if he wants some office woman rub down, the "G" train if he wants a school girl, and the "A" train for a good mixture of both. Today his choice is the #4 train!

He stands on the platform looking for that right person, the right situation to present itself. It's not a perfect science but if you get it right, you will be on a train with three or more women, that are looking for the same thing that is when he is at his happiest. Now the scene is set, its time to get down to his business! The train comes, he gets on with four women and two men in a car that couldn't hold three more. So he takes a position by the pole, a favorite of his. A woman blond hair, green eyes, and a nice little ass in that little business suit she was wearing, gets on.

He stands right behind her and she doesn't move away. This is the open door he's looking for! He puts his hand right on top of hers to simulate the position he would like to do with her, him on top pressing his whole body on her. She twists her hand to show just how she would grind her ass on him if given the chance. The train rocks, he bumps her with his dick, she doesn't move, O.K. That's the green light to turn things up. He moves as close to her as he can, giving her no place to back up and the pole is keeping her from moving forward. Now it's on!

He presses his dick on her as if they were at a club, slow music was playing. As his dick got hard, he could feel her pressing her ass on his dick as if she wanted it more than him. Wow what a turn on! He is so hard now that his dick is pulsating, and he can feel her ass tightening up as if she was trying to grab his dick with her ass cheeks. He's at the point now, all of this morning's work will pay off. He is so close he can feel her heart beat! He takes a good whiff of her hair and a look down at her tits that were oh so perky. Two stops pass and their still locked up grinding! He's thinking about sticking his dick in her ass then pussy, then ass then pussy, then ass then pussy, well you get the point.

She squeezes her ass, and he pulsates, and then bam, he explodes! She can feel his dick, rock hard then get soft, the whole time while squeezing her ass cheeks. She puts her hand down and gently rubs his dick, just to make sure there wasn't any more nut left. He gets off the next stop, and before he gets off the train, he looks back just to see if she felt what he did. And the look she gave him was, same time, same train tomorrow.

# 2

It's about 4:30pm and time to think about the ride home. She makes sure all of her paper work is done, cant loose this job. Her life is basically all about her job and her cat, Sam. Divorced for more than seven years but she tries to keep her head up, and not let every man that sees her, know she is as hot as a pizza oven! At forty-one, she finds alternative ways to get off. Like, looking at the bulge in a man's pants and wondering, what it would be like to ride him like a wild bull! Or look at a man's hands and think of him firmly grabbing her, forcing her to the ground and manhandling her until she cums hard enough to send the shuttle too the moon!

But on this day she craves for something extra. It's 5pm and its time to start the trip home. First a quick run to the bathroom, just to remove her panties, a girl has to be prepared to get a nut in public. Then she heads to the subway! She is a very young looking forty-one, but she is a little shy about meeting men. After being in an abusive relationship, she would rather be alone. So she likes to play with them instead. She takes her seat by the door, she likes one on one, her show is not for everyone, just someone special. Now with her eyes she starts undressing all the sexy men in her car, and today is special, it's loaded!

She puts her hand between her legs to catch the attention of the man sitting across from her. Then she opens her legs a little, to show him she has no panties on. As she looks at him as if he is the last dick on the planet, and she is ready as hell to procreate. She starts stroking her clitoris and rubbing her thighs, the placement of her over sized bag keeps, there encounter between them. While he looks at her licking his lips, as if to say I'm hungry enough right now to eat some pussy! She looks between his legs and sees his mid thigh dick, pointing due north! He gently rubs it to let her know, she is really getting to him.

Then she puts two fingers in, not to the point were anybody could see, as if she cared. Then she takes her hand out, and pretends to cough so she could sneak a taste. After licking her fingers clean, she put her fingers back, a little wet so she could feel it a little better. Now he's grabbing the head of his dick right through his pants. It was like they were fucking right in front of everybody, and no one knew! Then the moment of truth! She splashes down all over her hand, its so much it drips down her legs. Then she watches him grab that big ass bulge and squeeze it, until it exploded and left a stain on his pants. She gets off the next stop, I mean off the train.

She looks back at him and sucks the rest of the cum off her fingers, as if to say you next! And the look he gave her was, I wish what was in my pants was in your mouth!

# 3

So now you know what subway rider is all about!

Now lets get down to it, she's seventeen and nasty as hell, and willing to get her nut off anywhere and anyhow she can. She has those moments when she needs things, I mean special things. Like needing to get fucked in the ass, in and elevator. Having a threesome in the window in broad-daylight! Being tied up and whipped in front of an audience! But her all time favorite is, well let me tell you about it. This girl will get out of school and head to the subway, yeah you know. She finds her prey, and stalks them like a lioness on the prowl needing to feed her young!

She lets off some of her secret weapon, a little of her pussy juice in his location and watch him turn medieval. She leads him to the end of the platform and then she tells him that she has a problem. He replies what's the problem? She says well I'm only seventeen, and I mean well I have this thing that I like to do from time to time. He replies, well you're a very sexy young lady so I'm sure you could find someone to help you with that. Yeah you're right, I do have people for mostly anything, but a stranger can only do this. Wow! What's that? If I tell you promise you won't think I'm some nasty bitch! Baby what ever you have to tell me, trust, I won't think you're nasty.

O.K., well sometimes I like to go out and find a stranger and suck his dick on the train! Now what do you think about that? Yo! That's some shit. I mean what am I supposed to say? Here's my dick, suck it! Well not in so many words, but yeah. So they waited until most of the people left the station, she stood behind a pole and started rubbing his dick through his pants. While looking at other riders she would be stroking him and smiling, as if to say tomorrow you could be next. She waits until his dick gets rock hard. Then she bends down, and takes his dick out, she looks at it like it's the best thing since a bitch could breath! Meanwhile a man and his wife look on.

While hugging his wife from the back he whispers in her ear, that's some freaky, nasty, shit, we should be doing! She runs her hand up and down the shaft, squeezing when she gets to the head. She squeezes it at the shaft, than puts her lips gently on the head of his dick, he shakes, she says are you O.K., he says go head baby I'm good. She starts sucking him slow and deep, like they were not on a city subway platform. With one hand she holds his dick up, gently rubbing the crown, so she could get both of his balls in her mouth. She sucked them until they got soaking wet. Then she starts deep throating him, and gurgling on his dick, till he could not hold on any longer.

She looks him in the eye to let him know, don't hold back, I want it all! Then he came all over her face, and she did what any young freak would do. She licked up what ever she could, then sucked out what ever was left in his dick. She stood up and said to him that was good. With his dick still out, he said, that was the shit baby! I can hardly stand up, I never had my dick sucked like that before. Not my ex-girlfriends, ex-fuck buddies, current fuck buddies, hell, I paid a pro-ho to suck my dick, and that bitch, need to take some lessons from you. She said thank you, while licking some of the cum off of her lips, I do enjoy pleasing men.

He put his shit away and zipped up, she wiped her face, then turned around, and saw about seven or eight men and women that were watching them. He then said, are you O.K.? She said no! If I knew they were watching, I would have gotten real nasty!

# 4

Today I will tell you that I have been drunk and or high, and have been caught with my shit out of my pants, once or twice. But this guy I'm going to tell you about, takes show and tell to the next level. He wears his clothes baggier than he needs to, so he can protect his secret. Secret! What secret, you ask? The one he hides under his big hoodie. Ladies you ever seen a man on the train that appears to be sleep but he isn't. He's waiting for you! The one that's looking for something strange and unusual to see on the way home. So here she comes, thirty five to forty, and look's like she was the shit back in the days.

Her husband doesn't look at her, let alone touch her anymore! She sits down, looks him up and down, fixes her clothes and then sits back. He opens his eyes when the train stops, checks her out! He sees her thirty-eight double D's snuggled nice and tight in that thin sweater. Her thigh spreading on the train seat, like Jiffy on Wonder Bread! He notices her calf muscles are tight as a twenty-year-old sprinter. Then her eyes, deep and wanting, needing someone to let her know she can still get a man's dick hard, just because she's sexy! He fixes his clothes, opens his legs and gets ready to give her a show she will never forget!

He looks at her tits and thinks what it would be like to put his dick there. He sees her nipples getting hard, and that's when it happens. First she sees the head of his dick, she looks harder to make sure that's what it is. She tries to do it on the low, but her dick hungry ass couldn't help from licking her lips and rubbing her thighs. With all the seats on the train, she still doesn't move, that's when he goes full throttle. His dick rock hard and sticking out off his hoodie, and she's licking her lips and playing with her hair, letting him know you could put that big ass ten inch dick right here!

He gets so hard his dick starts to pulsate. She sees it and her nipples get so hard, it looked like they were going to rip right through her tight ass sweater. He looks her dead in the eye, and then he cums, without touching himself. I mean isn't that the ultimate big up for a bitch and her beauty. A man could find her so sexy he could fantasize about her and cum, without touching his dick, wow! He slumps down in his seat, and covers up. She gets off the train, says to him, thank you! I needed that, I got one too. On her way home she thinks to her self, I've been married for ten years, raising three kids, cook, clean and help pay bills.

And this son-of-a-bitch never thought I was sexy enough to cum just by looking at me. Maybe I should stop being a subway rider, and let someone on the subway ride me!

# 5

This story is about a thirteenyear-old boy, at a very strange point in his life. He has thoughts that he can't control, feelings he can't understand. He tries to talk to his dad, but his take on everything that goes on in the house is, tell your mother. His mom! Wow, you try telling your mother you have dreams of pissing all over a girl, while she kneels down before you. So he turns to his older brother, Mr. know everything, and do nothing. He tells him of this dream that he had about this grown lady, twenty-five years old. She had this sexy shirt on showing off her big ass tits. And she had these tight low cut jeans, with no draws on, just the thing to get a young man started. He said hello! She said hello back. He told her he thought she was the best-looking girl he had ever seen. She said thank you, then asked how old he was? He said I'm thirteen and a half, but I act older. She told him that was o.k. she liked young men.

Then said, I like being the first one to do things with a man. He said wow, I wish you were my girlfriend! She told him, I don't have a boyfriend right now, so anything is possible. They talked about his dreams, and she just looked at him and said I would love to fulfill your fantasy. She took him home, got undressed, kissed and licked all over him like he was a blow-pop, and she was looking for the cum, I mean gum inside! Then she got on all fours like a dog, an arched her neck so her face was right below his young and restless dick. Then she let him piss all over her face and back, while saying don't stop, this shit feels better than the shower I took this morning. His brother tells him that there is nothing wrong with it, as long as she liked it. So he feels if my brother said it was o.k. he must have done it, and he's fine, I guess. One night he finds himself on the train, tired and ready to go to sleep. It's a late night so not too many people were on the train, let alone in his car. He couldn't wait to find someone to have some fun with his new found freaky piss freedom he got from his brother.

He fell asleep for a minute, when he woke up, he saw a lady on the train by her self with her clothes half off. Like she was drinking all night with no care for what happens to her on the way home. From were he was sitting he could see her right nipple sticking out, he thinks, could this be any more perfect? He looks at her and notices, that she is a very sexy woman, if she wasn't past out on the train half naked, in a drunken comma! Then he stands up to see if anyone can see him from the other cars, just like in hide and seek, if you can't see them, they can't see you. Now standing in front of her he asks, are you alright? No reply.

Then he said excuse me Miss your tits are hanging out. Once again, no reply. He reached down and touched her nipple ever so softly, he didn't really want to wake her up. The train stopped, he knew he didn't have a lot of time, his stop was next. The doors closed, he took out his dick and started stroking it, and rubbing it on her tits. He got semi hard, then pissed all over her, while she was sleeping. She never got up, and he got off the train. It was good, but I wish she was awake so she could of had as much fun as I did.

# 6

Ah! What's next? Something I like to call spice. It allows me to feel there is something down the road worth living for. It's Friday just like any other Friday. She clock's out at the phone company, talks to some friends then begins her trip home. She stops for some chicken, two legs and medium coke. No one knows, but this woman has a secret, she is horny as hell! She sits by the front so she can see all the men walk by. She start's to eat her drumstick, when she sees this man six foot two, two hundred and fifty cut up pounds. Chocolate and fit, look like he could run the marathon with a bitch on his back.

She takes a slow deep bite out of her drumstick, you know at the top like she was sucking his dick. As he walks she watches his pant's bulge thinking what it would be like to be his suck slave. The shit got so good she drooled on her chicken, o.k. time to go. Feeling freaky for some strange reason, DICK-STICK! So she gets on the train pussy wet mouth wanting and ready to do some nasty shit. He leaves his job, just a mail clerk, at five p.m. like every day. He wonders what can he do to make his life a little better! It's dress down Friday so he had on his normal wear, basketball shorts, sneakers, and a shirt with some kind of sexual saying on it.

Like, "bad to the bone" with pictures of skeletons having sex, it was a very loose office. He would walk down the block looking at every ass from eight to eighty blind cripple and crazy. He would stop at the corner store, like usual, to see all the young pussy any man need to see. He stands on line watching these fine young things, bend over the counter and show off their happily new found, beautiful budding body parts. All this knowing a grown man is around and has no choice but to notice. A lot of men can say it, but not many men can be around such new tender pussy, and not get hard, and this guy was no different.

With his dick rock hard and pointing do north, stretching the fabric on those shorts to the limit. He enters the train, it's rush hour on a Friday and its crowded, but wait there's a lady sitting in a two-seater, with her bags in the seat like she was waiting for someone. He says excuse me, can I sit down? She looks up with her sexy eyes, smiles, then moves her bags. While sitting he notices that she is filling out her clothes like a prize horse fills out it's leather, just not as big! Sitting so close he could smell what perfume she put on that morning, and what she washed her hair with last night. He tells her he likes the way her hair smells, and could imagine smelling it while he slides deeply inside her from the back. She asked him, with your hands firmly on my neck, or waist? When we start off your waist, but the faster, the more aggressive I get, and I'm a beast when I'm behind an ass like yours. So yeah, I can see myself putting my hands firmly on your neck! She said yo, I hope you don't think I'm some sweet, shy, timid bitch, I like my dick 9 to 10 inches long, and two inches thick. Damn girl, can you put all that dick in your mouth, with out chocking? Only if you push my head down and make me! I mean when I get fucked I like to be dominated by a man, as long as he's a real man. What do you mean? I don't mind taking all that big dick punishment, but can a bitch sit on a nigger's face? I mean until a motherfucker like me drip all over your face and shit. He said you're like a dream come true, a fine ass freaky bitch, that's not afraid to tell a man just what she wants, even on a crowded train. By the way, what's your favorite position? Wow that's hard, I mean I like them all, but I love sixty-nine. Why? There is nothing better than to suck on some big ass meaty dick while riding a wet tongue, it just makes me feel like, like, like, well I don't know let's you and me try it? Well I'm getting off on the next stop, you could come home with me and let me fuck the shit out of you, with this mountain of meat.

Hey I always said I would suck my way to the top, I guess this is my chance, you lead I'll follow! Little did anybody know that this couple does this every once in a while just to keep things fun. SPICE!

# 7

This one should make you look for your daughter, and make damn sure she is not like this girl I'm going to tell you about. She's very young but definitely not shy. The type that can feel at home in a room full of horny young men, yes she has a dick fetish. I mean no matter what any body says she is going to get hers. A third generation freak, so her shit is deep. She stays on her knees, always ready to please, guys get back in line, cause the first nut was just a tease! The only thing that was off the list, was vaginal sex, she said that was for the man she would fall in love with.

But until then, she would let any man with a dick show her just how to be that slut every man wants to fuck. So if you have a dick, you too can put it in any hole you can fit in, besides the pussy. On this day for some reason she had to get something to make her even hornier. I'm talking about and "E" pill. If you don't know, I heard through the grapevine, that shit would make a Nun fuck the whole church, and love it! Well, anyway, she knew these two guys from school that knew where to get some. After school they met up. One of them told her, it cost five or ten dollars, depending on which one you want.

She said I want the best one for the best effect! They said OK, it's a long train ride you good with that? Yeah lets go! When they got there, they brought two. The man they got it from said, take half with some water and for no reason at all take a whole pill, it will take you places you don't want to go. Oh yeah, if you feel sick in any way after taking it, remember you don't know me! The two boys cut one in half, then downed it with a bottle of water. She looked at them, then said, you two are the cutest in the whole school so I want to make this special. Damn right! She took the whole pill. They went to a park to let the effect set in, it was Friday, so nobody had to be home anytime soon. Then she started to sweat, and then her young nipples got hard. She looked at the one with the sweatpants on and noticed his pole was pointing due north. And the other one kept kissing all over her and grabbing his rock hard dick. With a laugh she said lets go, I want to get it in on the train. That's what's up, let's go! They got on the train, horny as fuck, looking for a place to get it popping! It took a long time but they found this old storage room at the end of one of the platforms, it was dusty and not well lit, perfect! They snuck in unnoticed, now it's time to work off some of that sexual high. In like two seconds she was butt naked, with her hands on the top of the chair and her knees in the seat. The two boys positioned themselves, one in front and one behind. Switching at will, having as much fun as any young man would, sticking his dick from ass to mouth and back again. Until he comes mad times back to back, in her face, mouth, ass, can anybody give me a damn amen! It came to an end, she brushed her hair, put her clothes on, but didn't wipe her face off. One of them said hey, you forgot to wipe all our cum off your face! She said it's OK I'm happy to let everybody know I have twin dick snot on my face, it will make the ride home fun.

The two brothers looked at each other, and then got undressed for some more! They went at it for about four more hours, then passed out until the next morning when the workers found their naked cum drained asses.

# 8

As you can see in New York there is no reason for the Playboy Channel. If you have a good eye for sex in unusual places, you will have all the excitement you will ever need. With that said, this one is for the ages, I mean that quite literally. You know how people always say, how if you get married today, there is no chance for long-term sexual bliss, this couple kicked that shit to the curb. Married for more than fifty years, and still the apple of each other's eye's! Well into their seventies, and have meaningful sex at least three to four times a week. For people of that age it's a heavenly treat to have great, freaky, sex with one person for so long.

Hey, for some people their age just getting around is a challenge, let alone spending what little bit of energy they have left on fucking! He looks her deep in the eyes and says, I love all of your less than firm body, and every strand of your grey hair! It reminds me of just how long I have had your love, and it makes me want you more. She looks at him and replies, I have not known a man in my life that could hit all my spots like you! And your dick may be less hard now, but the width and length are still something an old bitch like me has to get ready for. Damn I love you! As they left the Broadway play she told him, let's take the train home.

Why, what's wrong with the Bentley? Nothing it's just that, this night is so perfect, I just don't want it to end! All right, you know I can't say no to you. They got on the train in the last car, sat in the two-seater at the end of the car by the conductor's room. She was kissing him on his ear and neck, and rubbing his thigh, his dick got hard then he said you know you can't fuck with him like that, he's gonna want some pussy! She looked down at his bulge, then grabbed and squeezed it, like only she could. Then the train shook, and he noticed the conductor's door was open. They looked at each other and said, one more time for old times sake.

He locked the door behind them, and put their coats over the window. He unbuttoned her shirt, to firmly grab, suck, and rub on her still nicely hung thirty-eight double de's. Then he opened up her skirt, it dropped to the floor, and he then slid his hands down her panties to feel that extra wet pussy of his. He put one of her legs up on the control box, so he could get a good angle, he's not that young any more. But she could still move well, from all those years of dancing and yoga. He gets on one knee an licks an sucks her pussy till she squirts all over his face and down his throat. Then he gets up and starts grabbing her ass and kissing all over her face.

He works up a good sweat, moving slow, then fast, then slow, then fast, until she cum's real hard, again! Then he says turn around, it's my turn! Ah shit daddy, give it to me! He pumped that old pussy so hard, he had her yelling like she was twenty-five. Then the big moment! She pushed him away, bent down to catch his load. Just like Foldger's, good to the last drop! They got dressed and started to leave the room, not realizing the train had reached the last stop and the conductor had called the police. But the police said to the, less than happy conductor, they have been married for fifty years, I hope I can get it that long, this good.

The conductor said hey, what about the smell of pussy all in my booth? The officer's reply, maybe this will make you go home and fuck your wife tonight! She looked at the officer and said, thank you. Not knowing she still had some of her husbands cum on her chin. Then she turned to her husband and said, hey honey this was much better than taking the Bentley home, you think we should sell it? They both said at the same time NAH!

# 9

The odd couple would be an under statement! First let me describe her. Five feet four inches, caramel skin, smooth like silk, with no other blemishes except some freckles. Light brown eyes, that were all hers, a sexy little button nose and perfect white teeth. Her breast was a very soft and perky 36C cup, with a nice slim twenty inch waist. Connected to hips you could put your drink on, and an ass you can put your plate on. Her shapely legs, brings you to her always pedicure toes, oh yeah, I forgot about her pussy, always shaved, ready for the eating! An overall beauty, at eighteen she is someone to cherish.

He was about six foot four, two hundred and sixty pounds. Not as fit as he should be, but his personality is great. The type of man who listens, because he really wants to know what's bothering you. He has a full beard, always trimmed, with a little salt and pepper. With a head full of curly hair, and grey eyes, just looking at him is enough to make a women wet. But his voice, wow! He had the sound of Barry White, with the sexiness of R. Kelly. Even at sixty-eight he was hung like a donkey, and knows just what to do with it. And did I mention he has a condo in mid-town, and drives a six hundred Benz!

One day they were having their usual Friday dinner, a pizza pie with everything on it, some hot wings, and a six pack of beer. She said baby, I have a fantasy, do you want to help me finally do it? Little mama you know I never told you no! Well I was just thinking what it would be like to fuck the shit out of you on the train. Now that's some shit I can fuck with, you heard! They got on the train at about one, one thirty and it was perfect. Yes there were a couple of people in the car they were in, but that didn't stop her. He had one of those I-pods with the speakers on it, playing the best in Hip-Hop and Reggae music.

She started off by giving him a very sexy lap dance, riding him pulling up her skirt showing off her tattoo, "hit that" on her naked ass. Then she got between his legs like she was going to give him some head right in front of everyone, rubbing her face on it and licking it right through his pants. The train car had only two other couples, a young man and women, and the other looked like they were married. Both couples looked at them like how could they do that in public, while secretly wanting to join in. He said, look hear little mama, take my dick out and sit on top. She did exactly what he said, and started ridding him like he was a prize bull at the rodeo, and she was going for first place. As the other couples watched, she looked at them and road him harder and harder, until she felt him nut real hard. She didn't stop grinding until his dick slipped out of her, she turned around to find out he was not awake. I guess the combination of pizza, pussy, and hot wings, was too much for his old heart. He suffered a fatal hart attack! Well I don't know about anybody else, but when I go, I hope I can cum in something young and sticky, then go! So guys if you see this pretty young thing with the tattoo (HIT-THAT) on her ass watch out, that's that killer pussy!

# 10

This one makes me say, can I join you guys please? I don't know about anybody else, but the idea of having sex with two sexy women is enough to drive a man fucking crazy.

Now I will say this, it's not all fun and games. It's hard to please two women to the point where they feel total bliss, not wanting any more dick. You must fuck one while keeping the other ones pussy wet by licking touching or fingering that shit. Then after you make the one your fucking cum, time to switch. You must be aware of the positions you can do, so everyone can get some at the same time. And you, as the man, you must hold your nut until they cum at least two times each! But things change based on the women your dealing with.

Like, lets just say if you have two straight women, you can't eat one while they eat one. Just by suggesting that it could fuck the whole night up. But if you're a real "G" you can swing it. Now the way I like it best is when one or both of the ladies are bi-sexual. In that situation you can do you, while letting the women do them. What do I mean you ask, let me tell you about it. I went to a Knicks game at the Garden, a little tipsy after a rare win, I started home. I got half way and had to get off the train, I needed to take a long hard piss. Now I wasn't looking for anything, I was fucked up and just ready to go home. When I looked around I didn't notice anybody except these two women that looked to be just sitting on the bench chilling. As I stumbled closer I notice one of them was sitting on the others lap, moving up and down. The one that was on the bottom had her hands all over the other ones tits. Me being the nasty mother fuck I am, I asked them did they need some help? They said at the same time, hell yeah! She stood up off of the seven inch strap-on she was ridding, and said I'm gonna put it on and fuck her so you can fuck me! They both had skirts on with no drawz, easy access!

There we were, her fucking her friend bent over the bench, and me fucking her. Then they both got on their knees and sucked my dick. After that, the one with the strap-on said, hey baby why don't you let him get that ass, while I hit that wet ass pussy. I sat on the bench, she eased her tight ass down on my dick, she got a nice rhythm, and then kicked her legs up on the bench to let her friend in. The one with the strap-on said, it's time I get some double penetration! We switched, I got the hardest nut I have ever got in my life, then past out. When I got up, my wallet and all my jewelry was gone. No girls, and not even a number, to get at them some other time.

Yes, I know what your thinking, they got me. Probably, but I still think I came out on top!

# 11

This I will say was a big ass disappointment! You know how you get when you see something that you're not ready for. Like, seeing someone you don't know throw up in public. That might make a person sick to there stomach, or lose there desire to eat food at that point. Or watching somebody getting beat up to the point where they are all bloody and shit. You may say to yourself, hey I know they fucked up, but I can't watch a person get beat to death! How about watching the history channel, on chemical warfare, and seeing all the people that have been affected by that type of cruelty. I would say man's worst moment in time, followed closely by the atom bomb!

Thankfully this story is not as serious as those, but to me still something shocking when you're not ready for it. Well getting down to it, I was where else, the subway! I was at 14$^{th}$ Street transferring to the "L" train, when I heard some moaning and slapping of flesh. So I stopped, listened, to see if I could hear where it was coming from. I walked slowly down the ramp because I thought that's where it was coming from. But when I got down there, I couldn't hear them anymore. Then I went back up, I could hear every stroke by the moan that was let out, as if he was killing that shit. If only I could catch them at the point of climax, that would be good by me.

Still hearing them, but not being able to find them, made me mad. I could hear them getting more into it by how fast the moaning got. I walked back to the "A" train station, but the only people over there was the clerk, two men looking at magazines and this bum sleeping on the floor. So I abandoned the search, and started on my way back to the "L" train. As I waited for the elevator I heard, fuck that ass damn it! The doors opened to my surprise, It was two men fucking! You know when they saw me they didn't stop! It was like they wanted me to see them. Me not being their type, walked away a little disappointed, at the fact there wasn't any pussy to see.

But the two men from the store, came as I walked down the stairs, and got in the elevator with them. So you see what might make one man sick, will give a hard-on to the next mans dick!

## 12

The New York Subway, oh how I love it and the people that work for it! M.T.A. workers are some of the hardest working people in the city! The subway never stops, so the good men and women that work for it never stop what they do, you dig. These two love to work over time, I guess you could say they are very dedicated in helping people get where their going. He's been with the company for almost twenty years as a token booth clerk. And as you may, or may not know, the M.T.A. has plans to get rid of the manned booths, and replace them with those electronic things.

That can't tell you where you're going, or call the police for you! Him being the worker he is, plans to show his supervisor that booths have some good value left, and without them the M.T.A. will not be able to serve the people as well. Now working the job isn't so easy! You have to stay awake in the middle of the night, when there isn't much to do, and that's when the supervisors like to come around. One night he had the same three to four people an hour, most of them his regulars. It was two thirty in the morning, time to clean up, count money, and take a nap.

Just as he was ready to dose off, his supervisor knocked on the door. He said hey what you doing out so late? She said my job, checking up on you! Wow do I look like somebody that wants to get paid for doing nothing, I love my Job. She said I know, I read your report stating that we shouldn't take people out of the booths. Well tonight I'm here to see if you could show me the value of having a man working in a booth by himself all alone. What do you mean? It's not hard to see how a man like you could have some fun late nights, if you wanted to. What kind of fun are you talking about? Hear me out for a second, if you wanted to you could have a woman in your booth sucking your dick, out of the sight of customers. But if I got caught, I'd get fired! Only if you got caught! I don't think I could find a woman that freaky for me to do that! If you look hard enough I bet you could find some co-workers that wouldn't mind. Yeah, like who? Well me of course! I work late but not this late, I came to fuck you, now what do you say to that? Are you trying to get me fired? No! The only thing I want from you is some nice stiff dick. Well being that you put it that way, hell yeah I want to fuck! But you know I can't leave the booth right. So what, I can stand up and let you hit it from the back, or let you sit on your stool and ride you, what ever you like.

He said first I want some head! She got down on her knees and started sucking him like super head. A customer came, and she was doing work I tell you! Spitting on the head, the deep throat special, making enough noise to make the customer say, hey, you OK man? When he left, she stood up so he could hit it from the back. Daisy was her name, so I guess he was riding Miss Daisy, but having way more fun than Morgan Freeman! With their pants down to their ankles a group of young ladies came up to the booth. They didn't have exact change, and they had big bills, so they had to stand for about a minute or two. While looking at the young ladies, his dick pulsating in her tight wet pussy. As they walked away he pulled out and came all over her apple bottom ass, with a Oh shit baby hear it comes! She rubbed it in and got dressed. Then said to him, I think I should make a recommendation to my bosses, to keep you guys in the booths, you serve the public well!

# 13

The New York subway, something special for everyone who rides. You have the women that are freaky, and ready for just about anything. And the men that are ready to find where and how to fuck in public. And those in the middle, that wish to be both, but are neither, so they just watch! But this guy I'm about to tell you about is one nasty mother, shut your mouth! Still he had all of the groups I mentioned above into what he was doing, no one called for help, the police, or anybody else that might make him stop. First I have to tell you about this guy. O.K. he was homeless, and had this gray wool trench coat on in the middle of the summer, one snakeskin shoe, missing a sole and strings. The other foot he had a slipper, showing off his ashy ass heels. He had a turtleneck sweater, and a little gold chain, like he might have been that guy back in the days! Oh yeah, he had some white dress pants on, held up by a rope, crazy right. About six foot, two hundred pounds, black as hell, a true Wesley Snipes look alike. I came through the gate, walked to the middle of the platform like I always do. It was me and about five or six women, and him. He was on the other side from me so unfortunately, I could see everything. At first he was just standing there, but when the women on his side got close to him, he pulled out like, Neno in New Jack City.

I'm not gay, but this nigger's dick was like the size of my arm! He started swinging it around like it was a cowboy's rope, then he got rock hard, and that's when the real bugged out shit happened. You know the women on his side walked closer too him, I guess to get a better look. As he stroked his dick, I could see some rubbing their tits, and playing in their hair, one even rubbed her pussy through her tight ass jeans. I guess seeing a real big dick for some women is the most important thing, fuck if he's clean, working, smart, or a good man. Even the women on my side walked over to watch, I can't lie, I was a little jealous.

When one of the women on his side walked up on him, he erupted like mount St. Helen, all over her skirt and shoes, she said oh my God! You make a bitch want to take you home, clean you up, and make you her man! Then they both left, with her leading him, while holding on to his dick! That day I wanted to quit my job, never wash, and take those enlargement pills, ya heard!

# 14

High school, what a time for learning and exploring ones sexual talents. What your good at, what you like, and most of all whom you could do it to! Sometimes it is as hard as finding the solution for "X" in a math problem, or when to and how to use to or too, in a sentence. But when you find the right person that can help you grow and build on your own freaky nature, without making you feel funny about trying new things, that is your sexual guide, i.e., your teacher! These encounters started without planning, or any attempt to hurt anyone. But as in all good stories, yes somebody is going to have their feelings hurt and their heart ripped out of their chest.

Oh yeah and jail is not out of the question! Now this young man was seventeen and somewhat of a social outcast. Very smart but too cool for the geeky kids, not athletic so he couldn't hang with the jocks, not a fighter so the tough crowd, not an option, and a look the ladies would have to get to know him too like him. It started with a simple good morning, how was your day today? Then some licking of the lips, with eye contact, and a gentle rubbing of her chest on his back in class. For her it was the ultimate taboo! Thirty-two, married with children, happy on the outside, sad on the inside. She fell into this due to his innocence and pure heart.

Able to tell a lie, but refuses too! Saying I love you to him is not just a statement, but also more like a way of life. By his senior year it had got so bad they knew they had to do something about it, more than what they had. Knowing they couldn't get caught, they came up with new ways to fuck all the time. Like after school help, one on one! Showing up late after basketball and cheerleader practice, for a nice hot shower together. But this was the day they regret, one that led them to take their little fling thing public, yes the subway! They left school, went to the subway, and waited for the most crowded train they could find, and then got on.

She had on her business suit, with the split up the ass, as usual, he had baggy jeans and a white "T" on. They went to the end where you walk through the cars by the conductor, he pulled out his dick, and she pulled up her dress! Just enough to get his dick through the split. They bumped and grind for three stops until she came, and as he was pulling out, with his cum shooting everywhere, they saw two kids from their school filming them on their camera phone. At that point they knew their lives were over. It was all over U-tube the next day, and the day after that the Dean saw it, and the day after that her husband found out, and the day after that the police found out.

So as you see one had his heart broken, because he couldn't be with the woman he loved, and the other one went to jail for sex with a minor. Now for you teachers and students that want to get it on, personally I have no problem with that, just stay off the public subway and you'll be fine.

# 15

Sometimes in life we get with people that we don't know, and later on find out we need more! With this couple I would say neither one knew what the other person's sexual needs were, but still they were in love. They met in high school, she was the best looking girl in the whole school. Every guy wanted her, so anybody who got with that, and kept it, was the shit! He was the captain of the football team, so he had his fair share of little high school bitches. Yo, on prom night they were like royalty! Everybody said they were the couple to most likely make it, money, love, and kids, anything they wanted they could have.

Now lets push forward ten years, four kids, a sixteen point five percent, and rising mortgage. Oh yeah, and a car payment that was so much, they couldn't put gas in it, so they took the, what else, the subway all the time! If you are, or ever have been married, you know sometimes you can get caught doing shit you got no business doing. Well now you know somebody is going to cheat! But first let me tell you about the person they cheated with. She was five foot tall with long jet black hair, and if apple bottom means you have a nice ass, this bitch had a watermelon bottom, the bigger the fruit the better the juice.

Her face, are you kidding, it was like Jada Pinkett Smith meets, Lisa Ray, complete with the fuck me eyes and smile to die for. Her tits were perfect, I mean you could tell through her shirt and bra those shits sat up just right! And her legs were short but very shapely, rapped in that mocha colored skin. He met her one-day coming home from work, and just couldn't let her go. He told her he had a wife and kids, she told him that was something she didn't need to know. I mean you just want to fuck me right? Damn, how can you be so fucking bad and so to the point, it's like a dream! If you let me fuck you and that's all I can get, I would have no problem with that.

But I got to tell you, my wife is on my ass every minute of the day, it's hard to get out the house after work. She said baby I'm easy like Sunday morning, you can have this pussy where ever, and when ever you see me! Well the only time I see you is on my way home from work, on the train. I will say even for a freak like me that shit is a little out there, but I want to fuck you so bad, I'll let it go down. The day came and she was ready for it! Her out-fit was a see through top with some spandex pants, no drawz! He got off work, rushed to meet her, they went to a place he noticed a while ago where the trackmen put their tools. They went in and got into the back office, then got busy.

She sucked his dick so good his whole body was shaking! Then he put her back on the desk, and ate that pussy until she came like five or six times. She had cum all down her legs, and the crack of her ass and shit. Then he started fucking the shit out of her! I mean he did the seizer, cowgirl, reverse cowgirl, doggie, butterfly, sixty-nine standing up, and every long dick position he could before he came all over her tits and stomach. Now remember I said someone could get caught doing something wrong. Well it was his anniversary, and his wife went to his job to take him out.

She had planned to walk up on him in the train, but when she saw him and her she followed them, and watched the whole thing! When her husband walked out of the office, she was standing there with no pants on, pussy wet as hell. He said what the fuck! She said no reason I couldn't have some fun, I see you were. You know if you wanted some more pussy, you could have told me, I like pussy too! He said baby I never knew, you sure you're not mad? A little, but she is so fucking bad, I want some too. Oh yeah, I was going to take you out and get that phone you wanted for our anniversary, but you got your gift, lets go home. It's my turn to see what she taste like!

# 16

Hey, you ever saw that show a few years ago called, young doctors in love? This story is nothing like that, but there is a young doctor, and he is looking for love, or anything close. Picture this, a man with his whole life together yet he can't find a good woman. In college he was the overachiever, never partied, and you can be damn sure he never dated anyone. Part of it was he came from a poor family, so he had to make it, everyone counted on him. The other part was he was more then just a little shy. One day on the way back from class, a young lady came up to him and said, I've been watching you for some time now.

I know you don't have a girl at school, so I guess you love the one you have at home a lot. I mean, that type of loyalty is just what a bitch like me is looking for. You don't have to love me like that, just let me be the only one down here you're fucking, and I will fuck and suck you like I was your wife! He said no I don't have anyone, anywhere, so you don't have to worry about the next girl. So the dick is all mine, I don't have to share it with anybody! She said, you don't know how happy you just made me. Well, I never had a girl come at me like this in my life before, I really don't know what to do.

It was nighttime so she said, yo, come with me to those bushes so I can make this official. What do you mean? What else, I'm going to suck your dick and swallow all that hot and sticky cum! He was so excited at the chance that he was going to get his dick sucked, for the first time, he came before they got to the bushes! When they got to the spot and she took out his dick and saw that he came, she laughed, and said, if you came that quick there is no way you can fuck me like the bitch I am. Good bye! Oh, when you see me, act like you don't!

Now any sex therapist will tell you, that type of encounter may have long lasting problems.

This day he was on the "D" train, on his lonely way home, when the train got stopped between two stations. Not important to him he was in no rush. Then one of the passengers passed out! He told everyone, back up I'm a doctor! When he got to the person he saw it was the best looking women he had ever seen. She had a 40DD cup that was all hers, with a six-pack. He could see that because she only had on a tank top, with some spandex shorts, like she was working out today. You know a girl has a fat ass when her back arches up off the floor like eight inches. He kneeled down beside her and started to do C.P.R., when he found his dick getting hard.

Yeah, he tried to stay professional but he just couldn't fight the feeling. He put his hands together to start pushing down on her chest, while rubbing his dick on her leg. Then he arched her head back to clear the air pathway, held her nose, opened her mouth, then gave her a nice breath of air, with a little tongue on the side. By the time he gave her the third one, she woke up! Feeling his hard dick beside her, and wanting to thank him for saving her life, she slipped him her number and a kiss. Then she told him, in his ear, I was awake for two of those breath kisses! But when I peeked at you, you looked so good and determined to save me, plus I could feel how hard you were. I said to myself, I've got to give this man some pussy, he earned it! Then the train started to move, she held his hand as they left the train, and everybody cheered! It's about time our young doctor in lust got his nut off, in some pussy for a change.

# 17

The one thing I can say is if you need to fuck, the M.T.A. provides more than enough time and space for way less money than any hotel in the city. But the risk of being seen doing something private and personal may be too much for the average person, but in New York as you can see, we don't have too many average people. The people in this story are a little crazy, a little horny, and a little bold, you could say they are a little of a lot of things, except little! You know when you're a man and you can't see your own dick because of your own stomach, you're too big to have sex in public. So can I say no shame in his game!

He is about two hundred and fifty to three hundred pounds, if you like big boy loving he got it good. Now his girlfriend is at lease his size or bigger! I guess it looks that way because she has real big tits, and a big old fat shapely ass. You know the type of ass you could just lie on and loose your self in. She is just as much the freak as he is, often suggesting weird and unusual sex. With them it isn't just being seen by people that get them off, it's the danger! I mean he works as a welder in high-rise buildings, and one day after work they had sex out on one of the beams. She was standing up by one of the beams with just her top on tits out and bent over.

He fucked her so hard that day they almost fell off! Lots of people like to fuck in the rain, but these two went to Central Park during a storm, complete with high winds, heavy rain and yes, lightning! Now picture two big people butt naked rolling around in the mud, fucking. This one time they went on a vacation to Arizona, rattle snake country, and just had to have sex out in the open dessert. But this day the two had to out do anything they had done or probably will ever do! Sex on the train and sex on the platform, I can understand, but in the tunnel, are you crazy! I guess for sex thrill seekers it's the ultimate get off, if you survive.

He had on his work clothes, so it looked like he worked down there. They went to a storage room and took off all their clothes, then got in the middle of the tracks. He put his hands up on the beams while she bent down and sucked his dick. Then she turned around and let him hit all that ass while trains kept passing. And whenever someone saw them, she would wink and smile at them. Not stopping for nothing, even when the trains past by and sparks from the third rail hit them, he just fucked her harder! Just before he came they could hear someone coming, so he pulled out so they could go get dressed. But she told him, I came like five times baby, you know I can't leave owing you!

So she sucked out the biggest nut he ever gave her. I mean all over her face, eyes, mouth, you know the perfect cum face. She had so much in her eyes she couldn't see where she was going, so when they started running to get dressed, she ran right into the men that where coming. They gave her something to clean off her face, she said thank you, and I guess I should go get my clothes. At that time she heard her man call to her, the workers said you know you could get killed down here! She said I know that's the thing, get as close too death before cuming.

# 18

This is as funny as it is sad. I mean if I had a physical problem that would prevent me from having a fair chance to defend myself or know when danger is coming, I would stick to doing private things in private. What I'm saying is, if I had one short arm I wouldn't go around telling people I'm going to knock you out. And if I was a midget, I wouldn't be saying I'm going to kick your ass, can you feel me! Yes sometimes having a disability works in your favor, like Stevie Wonder, he can't see but he learned to play and perform music. But if he couldn't hear, what would his shit sound like? Shit! This couple is what they must have meant by the blind leading the blind.

Lets take the man in this case first, in his thirties and blind from birth, so he is fully adapted to life without sight. In some ways he thinks of himself blessed, to not see all of the real bad shit that goes on. His other senses are much better than you and I, like smell and touch. Hey I wonder if that works for his dick, might make a freak like me, fuck blindfolded! You know people that can't see always bug me out when they count money, like come on, how do they know one bill from the other. Now his girlfriend for the last three years just lost her eyesight eight years ago. She can do some things by herself, but she likes to rely on him for things, like counting money and navigation.

Can I take you there? Two blind people at the ticket machine, take out their money count what they need, wait for their change and metro cards. Then they get to the turnstile, use the metro card without any problem, a little better than some people that can see. They get down the stairs and stand at the end of the platform, he reads the Braille sign when his girl says to him, baby I'm horny as hell! I mean what do you want me to say, you didn't want any dick at the house so why now? I don't know, but I do, can't you smell how wet my pussy is? So what the hell, you want me to just take out my dick and start fucking you right here! No!

I was thinking maybe, we could find a closet or storage room, and use that. Baby if you didn't know, I'm here to tell you, I'm blind! But you hear better than anybody I know. What if we get caught going in? Just wait till you can't hear anybody or smell anybody. O.K. let me look for a place, but if I can't find one on this platform, we're getting on the train! They went from one end to the other, and wound up walking right into a door. He turned the doorknob, it was open, and then they waited. When the coast was clear, they went in. After waiting so long she was as hot as an oil fire, and no foam anywhere, I guess hot cum will have to do!

I mean she sucked his dick like only a woman with a good touch could. Grabbing on it and feeling all over it, like it was a big ass banana she had to peel, then eat! While he felt every touch, suck, and lick to the tenth power. Then he picked her up and fucked the shit out of her standing up, with his hands all on her ass and shit. She came all over him like she was a virgin, at thirty-two. He then turned her around and fucked that ass, until she couldn't take it then he came. She jerked his dick until no more cum came out, then they got dressed. Now the room they found was the police booth, sound proof and half glass all around!

So they couldn't hear anybody, and you know they couldn't see anybody, but people saw them. As they walked to their train, people clapped, and yelled out, hear no evil, see no evil!

# 19

Every time I close my eyes I have these freaky thoughts of sex with people I don't know, or them having sex, I mean hot nasty sex! What do you mean? Don't ask! Just tell me. O.k. if that's what you want, here it is. When I was in high school, I had fallen a sleep and had a dream about my whole class. The girl next to me was a pretty little chocolate thing with a nice fat, round, bouncy ass. She was getting fucked in the ass and then sucking her ass cum off all the guys that wanted some of her ass that day. The two troublemakers in the back were fucking the shit out of this bad ass Spanish girl.

They were fucking her ass, mouth, and pussy, I mean they were flipping that bitch like she was a pancake at IHOP! And they even had a cum tasting line. It was these three bitches straight out of a SWEETS magazine in the front of the class, jerking niggas off into a bowl, and then tasting it too see who had the best dick snot! Wine testers don't have shit on them. The teacher even got into it. She was giving out grades based on how hard you made her cum. One got you a "B", a real hard one got you the "A", but if you could give her multiple orgasms you got the "A+". One day I was at church and I fell asleep, you know what I was thinking should have sent me straight too hell, thank goodness my lord let me get away with that! So I can't give details, you never know how many chances you get with him, just know this, it was as bad as it gets. Now we get to today, sleepy, horny, and on the train, where else would I be in this story! There had to be like thirty people on the train. It wasn't real crowded but it wasn't empty by no stretch of the imagination. I got a corner seat and fell out into this sexual comma like sleep. One of the guys had a radio and started playing some stripper music and all the women started dancing on the poles and taking off their clothes. This girl took her panties off right in this mans face, he spread her ass cheeks and started eating that pussy. Another man had this badass chick, I'm saying her ass was so fat and round, the shit should be in magazines. And he was fucking the shit out

Edwards Brothers Malloy
Thorofare, NJ  USA
June 12, 2013

of her, in doggie style, yes on all four knees on the train. Her pussy was so wet you could hear it making that fart sound as he pounded that fat ass. One of the women on the train made a train, a dick sucking train! Niggas were sticking their dicks in her mouth cumin and moving on, and she didn't care as long as the next one was put in her mouth. This one woman was riding this man in her ass, it must have been her first time because she was screaming at the top of her lungs, like he was killing her.

Then someone came over and put their dick in her mouth to shut her up! These three women had this one man that had fucked them so much he fell out, and they never stopped sucking his dick waiting for him to get hard again. Yes there was this man-dingo motherfucker that must have had a fourteen-inch dick! Yo, no shit, he was fucking this little bitch and had two other bitches sucking the rest of his dick that wouldn't fit. The shit got so good to me that when the conductor tapped me to get me up, my jeans were stuck to me from all the cum in my pants.